Dear Parent:

Congratulations! Your child is taking the first steps on an exciting journey. The destination? Independent reading!

STEP INTO READING® will help your child get there. The program offers five steps to reading success. Each step includes fun stories and colorful art. There are also Step into Reading Sticker Books, Step into Reading Math Readers, Step into Reading Write-In Readers, Step into Reading Phonics Readers, and Step into Reading Phonics First Steps! Boxed Sets—a complete literacy program with something for every child.

Learning to Read, Step by Step!

Ready to Read Preschool–Kindergarten
• big type and easy words • rhyme and rhythm • picture clues
For children who know the alphabet and are eager to begin reading.

Reading with Help Preschool–Grade 1
• basic vocabulary • short sentences • simple stories
For children who recognize familiar words and sound out new words with help.

Reading on Your Own Grades 1–3
• engaging characters • easy-to-follow plots • popular topics
For children who are ready to read on their own.

Reading Paragraphs Grades 2–3
• challenging vocabulary • short paragraphs • exciting stories
For newly independent readers who read simple sentences with confidence.

Ready for Chapters Grades 2–4
• chapters • longer paragraphs • full-color art
For children who want to take the plunge into chapter books but still like colorful pictures.

STEP INTO READING® is designed to give every child a successful reading experience. The grade levels are only guides. Children can progress through the steps at their own speed, developing confidence in their reading, no matter what their grade.

Remember, a lifetime love of reading starts with a single step!

For Griffin—may you always fly home!
—M.L.

To Elizabeth Morris
—H.W.

Published in the United States by Random House Children's Books,
a division of Random House, Inc., New York.

STEP INTO READING, RANDOM HOUSE, and the Random House colophon are registered trademarks of Random House, Inc.

www.randomhouse.com/kids
www.stepintoreading.com

Educators and librarians, for a variety of teaching tools, visit us at
www.randomhouse.com/teachers

Library of Congress Cataloging-in-Publication Data
Loehr, Mallory.
Dragon egg / by Mallory Loehr ; illustrated by Hala Wittwer. — 1st ed.
p. cm. — (Step into reading. Step 1)
SUMMARY: A dragon's egg rolls out of its nest in a cave, continuing along a road, past a castle, and through a town, where it bumps against a rock and cracks.
ISBN: 978-0-375-84350-1 (trade)
ISBN: 978-0-375-94350-8 (lib. bdg.)
[1. Eggs—Fiction. 2. Dragons—Fiction.] I. Wittwer, Hala, ill. II. Title.
PZ7.L82615Dr 2007
[E]—dc22 2006027015

Printed in the United States of America

10 9 8 7 6

First Edition

Dragon Egg

by Mallory Loehr
illustrated by Hala Wittwer

Random House New York

Dragon eggs in a nest.

Dragon mama takes
a rest.

One egg tips.

Then it rolls.

The egg rolls
out of the nest!

The egg rolls
out of the cave.

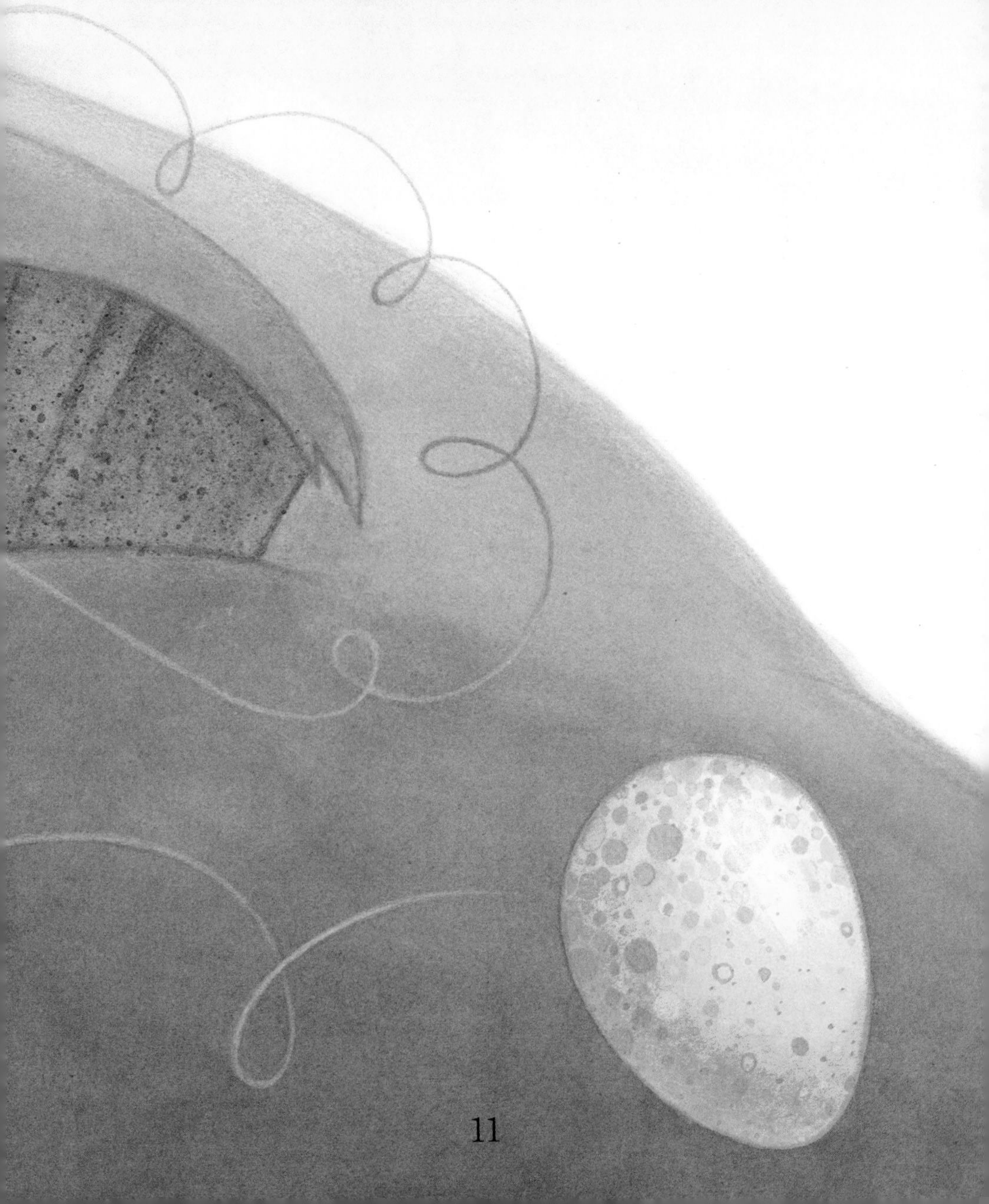

The egg rolls
down the hill.

The egg rolls
along the road.

The egg rolls
past a castle.

The egg rolls
through a town.

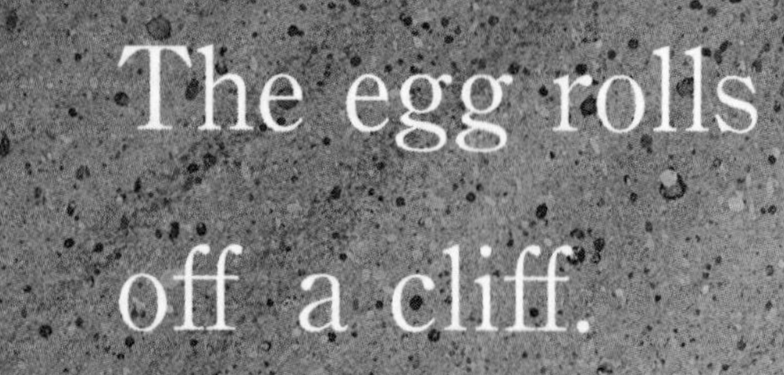

The egg rolls
off a cliff.

BANG!

The egg cracks open!

The baby dragon opens his mouth. . . .

Pfff!

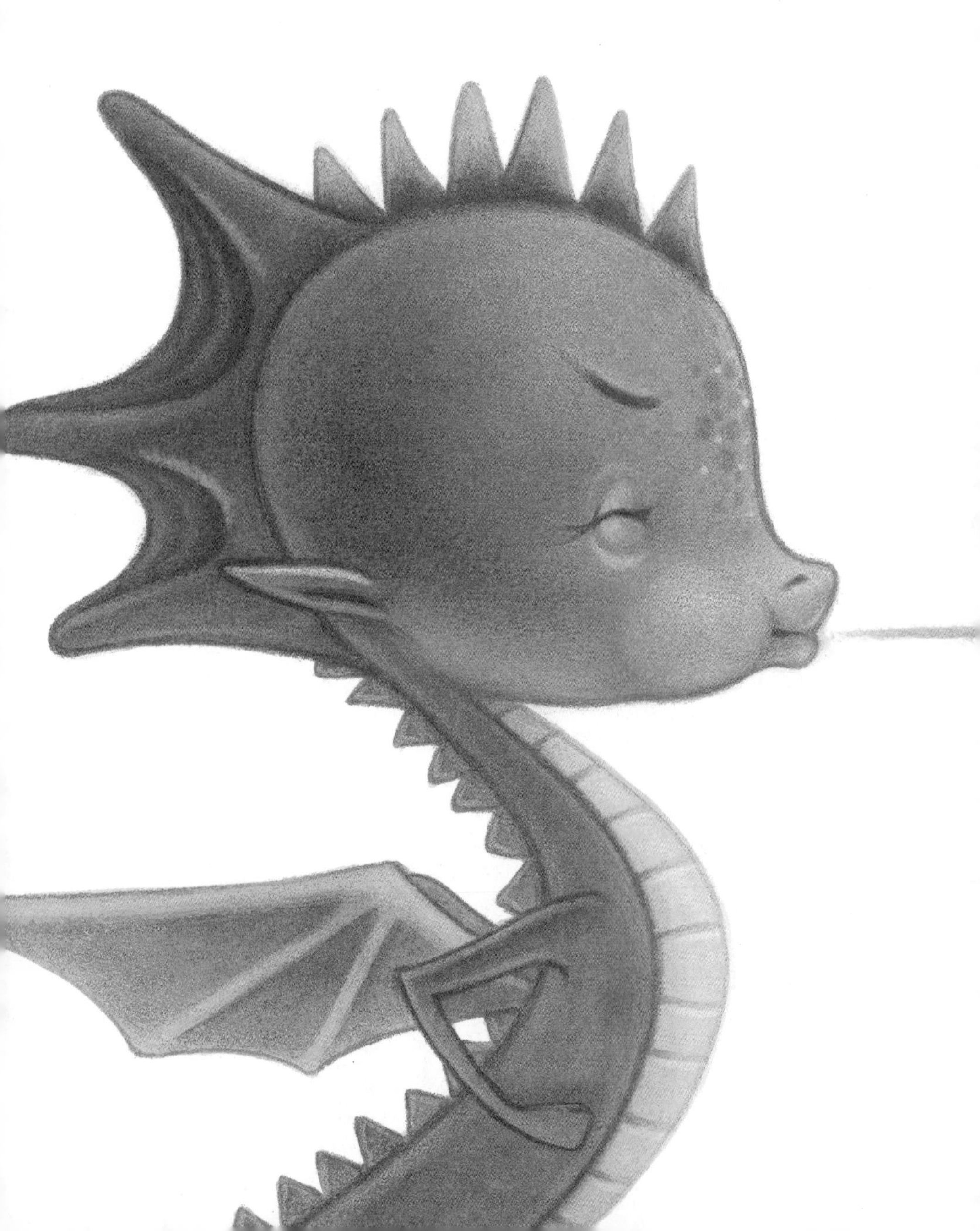

Out comes a little fire!

The baby dragon flies
through the town.

The baby dragon flies
past the castle.

The baby dragon flies
along the road.

The baby dragon flies
up the hill.

The baby dragon flies into the cave.

Look who is waiting!